Borscht and Beyond

ಏ

LOUISE PEPPER

authorHOUSE®

AuthorHouse™
1663 Liberty Drive
Bloomington, IN 47403
www.authorhouse.com
Phone: 1-800-839-8640

First published by AuthorHouse 9/14/2009

ISBN: 978-1-4490-2592-2 (e)
ISBN: 978-1-4490-2591-5 (sc)

Printed in the United States of America
Bloomington, Indiana

This book is printed on acid-free paper.

Creator Comments

What began as a curiosity of an ancestral peasant soup and its many origins, rapidly became an infatuation with a much overlooked tuber, mostly Burgundy, (although she does live in other colors) The Queen of Root Vegetables. *The blushing Bride as it were.* Created more for whimsey, sharing information and food for the soul than culinary greatness.

After the completion and publication of the Great Canadian Chicken, a most delightful and interesting journey, my next mission was to write that Grrreat Canadian Novel. Somewhere along the way, I veered back to cooking. I have always enjoyed cooking, entertaining and exploring or creating new recipes. However, I thought I needed to move in to a more worldly direction. A novel, of great interest and so much verbosity that it would become a Best Seller overnight! Somewhere along the way there, I became involved with a beet. You might say began with a Bowl of Borscht.

The more I researched and gathered Beet bios and applications, the more I became obsessed. What fun to discover that what my Mother grew so successfully in her garden, and cooked with such dedication, was one of the healthiest foods on this planet earth. Guided only by her ancestral heritage, and natural outstanding cooking skills, She raised a healthy spunky family. Could have been the **Beet**, seasoned with good parenting skills.

It is a pleasure to be able to share this book of *Beetisms*, so that you too may expand your joy of this wondrous vegetable. The reason for the title Borscht and Beyond........ well, it will evolve as you read on.

The sequel to this exploration may well be the **Beyond** Borsch that beets are regularly used for.

Welcome to world of .... *Beta vulgaris*
Scientific Name: *Beta vulgaris*

Beet History

Beets, botanically-known as *Beta vulgaris*, are native to the Mediterranean. Although the leaves have been eaten since before written history, the beet root was generally used medicinally and did not become a popular food until French chefs recognized its potential in the 1800's. Beet powder is used as a coloring agent for many foods. Some frozen pizzas use beet powder to color the tomato sauce. The most common garden beet is a deep ruby red in color, but yellow, white, and even candy-striped (with red and white concentric circles) are available in specialty markets. It is estimated that about two-thirds of commercial beet crops end up canned. Beets are available year-round with prime time being from June through October.

Beauty & the Beet

Beets are so bashful they keep their heads in the ground. You don't hear much about them. People rarely serve them. As a matter of fact, in the world of vegetables, beets are seldom even mentioned. However, we revere them so much that we've taken them from their home in the ground to place them "On the Highest Perch" for special recognition.

Beets would never boast of their many health benefits without a little coaxing. Beets, also known as beet root, are high in potassium, folacin, and fiber, yet low in calories. Their edible leaves offer protein, calcium, fiber, beta carotene, vitamins A and C, and some B vitamins. They're known in the arena of natural healing for their ability to purify the blood and the liver. Beets make lasting friends almost instantly. Once you've tasted fresh beets in the peak of their season, you'll delight in their sweetness and versatility. We should mention that they have one of the highest sugar contents of all in the vegetable kingdom. They can be eaten raw, boiled, steamed, roasted, or saute. If you visit farmer's markets on a regular basis, you might be able to take home some of the specialty varieties that are harvested early in the season, such as Baby Beets and Golden

Beets. While beets are at their best in season, they are available throughout the year because they store well. Avoid the exceptionally large ones, or you'll be chewing on woody cores with little sweetness.
roasting.

BORSCHT a soup from Eastern Europe made with fresh beets, assorted vegetables, and sometimes with meat and/or meat stock, usually garnished with a dollop of sour cream and served either hot or cold.

The Beet and its International Friends join flavors to delight your palate......

Russian Palace Vegetable Borsch

1 Tbsp vegetable oil
1-1/2 cups onion, finely chopped (1 large)
5 medium beets
1/2 cup carrot, chopped (1 small)
5 tsp tomato paste
16 cups chicken stock
2 large potatoes
1 medium cabbage head
1 cup green bell pepper, chopped
3 Tbsp sugar
1/3 cup lemon juice, fresh squeezed
1 tsp salt
1/2 tsp ground black pepper
1 clove garlic, minced
1 tsp fresh dill weed, chopped

Peel and julienne raw beets to yield 4 cups. Peel and cube potatoes to yield 2 1/2 cups. Finely chop cabbage to yield 6 cups.

Heat oil in a large skillet over medium-high heat. Add onion and saute until browned, about 5 to 7 minutes.

Add beets and carrot. Saute, stirring constantly, for 10 minutes.

Stir in tomato paste. Remove from heat and set aside.

In a large stock pot, bring chicken stock to a boil over high heat. Add potato and cook for 3 minutes. Add cabbage and continue boiling for 5 minutes. Add reserved beet-tomato paste mixture, green pepper, sugar, lemon juice, salt and black pepper. Reduce heat to a simmer and cook for 15 minutes. Remove from heat. Stir in garlic and dill. Serve hot.

Chilled Beet and Watermelon Soup

1 Tbsp vegetable oil
1 medium onion, peeled and sliced
1/2 pound **beets**, peeled and roughly diced
4 cups chicken stock OR low-sodium chicken broth
1 tsp salt
2-1/2 cups diced seeded **watermelon** (rind removed)

Heat oil in a stock pot over low heat. Add the onions and cook slowly, stirring, about 7 minutes. Add the beets and continue to cook slowly, covered, until most of their water has been released and they have fallen apart, about 35 minutes. Stir often to avoid sticking and burning.

Add the stock and salt, cover and bring to a boil. Reduce the heat and simmer, covered, for 15 minutes. When the soup is finished cooking, strain and reserve the liquid. Transfer the beets to a blender or food processor and add the watermelon. Puree until very smooth. Return the puree to the pot and add the reserved liquid, mixing to combine. Chill the soup well, about 4 hours before serving.

Cream of Beet Soup

1 lb beets, peeled and coarsely -chopped (about 3 medium)
1 lrg onion, coarsely chopped
1 Fresh marjoram sprig
  -OR
1 tsp. Dried of chopped fresh thyme
3 Tbsp Unsalted butter
1 qt. Chicken or vegetable broth
1/2 cup Heavy cream
2 Tbsp Good red wine vinegar
Salt
Pepper
1/2 c up Heavy cream, lightly whipped
Small croutons
1/4 cup Chopped fresh herbs, such -as dill or marjoram

Cook beets, onion and marjoram in butter in a 4-quart pot over medium heat until onion begins to soften slightly, about 10 minutes. Add broth, partially cover pot, and simmer slowly for about 30 minutes,until beets are completely soft. Check them by trying to crush one against the side of the pot with a wooden spoon. Simmer longer if necessary.

Puree soup in a blender or food processor. If you want soup to have a smoother texture, strain it through a medium-mesh strainer. Add cream of vinegar and bring soup back to a simmer. Season with salt and pepper

To serve, ladle into bowls and garnish with whipped cream, croutons and herbs, or serve garnishes separately and let diners help themselves.

Hearty Russian Beet Soup

1 c Navy beans, dry
2-1/2 lb Lean beef
1/2 lb Slab bacon
10 cups Cold water
1 Bay leaf
8 Whole peppercorns
2 Cloves garlic
2 Tbsp Dried parsley
1 Carrot diced
1 Celery stalk diced
1 Large red onion chopped
Salt to taste

8 medium Beets for soup
2 cups Red cabbage, shredded
2 Large leeks, sliced
3 Med.potatoes, cut Into eighths
1 can crushed tomatoes
1 tb Tomato paste
3 tbsp Red wine vinegar
4 tbsp Sugar
1 lb Kielbasa (opt)
2 tbsp Flour
1 tbsp Butter, melted
1/2 cup Sour cream (opt)

Cover beans with water and allow to soak overnight; cook until tender; drain; set aside. Place beef, bacon and water in large soup pot; bring to a boil. Skim fat from surface. Add bay leaf, peppercorns, garlic, parsley, carrot, celery, onion and salt. Cover and simmer over low heat for about 1 1/2 hours. Scrub beets for soup and cook in boiling water until tender, about 45 minutes; drain and discard water; cool. Peel and cut each beet into eighths. Scrub small beets; grate; cover with water to soak.

Remove meat from soup; set aside. Strain soup into another pot and add cooked beets, cabbage, leeks, potatoes, tomatoes, tomato paste, vinegar, sugar, beef and bacon. Bring to a boil and simmer 45 minutes.

Cut kielbasa into chunks and add with navy beans to soup. Simmer 20 minutes more. Mix flour and butter together to form paste. Stir into soup to thicken slightly. Strain raw beets, saving liquid and discarding beets. Add beet liquid to soup.

Additional sugar or vinegar may be added for sweeter or more sour flavor. Slice meat and arrange in individual soup bowls. Pour hot soup with vegetables over meat. Garnish each serving with a dollop of sour cream, if desired.

Red Onion and Beet Soup

2 tsp. olive oil
1-1/2 cup red onions, sliced
2 garlic cloves, crushed
1 – ½ cup cooked beets, cut into sticks
5 cups vegetable stock or water
1 cup cooked soup pasta or barley
2 tbsp. raspberry vinegar
salt
black pepper
low fat yogurt and chopped chives, to garnish

Heat the olive oil and add the onions and garlic Cook gently for about 20 minutes or until soft and tender. Add the beets, stock or water, cooked pasta shapes and vinegar and heat thoroughly. Adjust the seasoning to taste. Ladle the soup into bowls. Top each one with a spoonful of yogurt and sprinkle with chopped chives. Serve piping hot. Serves 6.

Cook's Tip: If you prefer, try substituting cooked barley for the pasta to give extra nuttiness.

Washington Borsch

4 medium beets
2 cups vegetable stock
4 chopped shallots
5 sprigs of sage
Cheese:
1/2 cup (125 ml) soft goat cheese
2 chopped shallots
2 chopped garlic cloves
Salt and pepper

Boil beets in salted water until tender (about 2 hours). Peel beets while still warm and put in a blender. Add warm stock, shallots, and sage and blend until smooth. Strain through a sieve and keep warm.
Mix goat cheese with shallots and garlic, and add salt and pepper to taste.
Form cheese mixture into quenelle shapes.
In soup plates, center a quenelle and ladle soup gently around it.
Garnish with a julienne of sage.

Beets and Greens and Sweet Potatoe Soup
(Pressure Cooked)

5 medium beets with greens attached

3 medium sweet potatoes (about 1 1/2 lbs) .. peeled

2 tablespoons unsalted butter

2- 1/4 teaspoons finely minced fresh ginger --

1 large onion -- coarsely chopped

6 cups vegetable stock -- or bouillon

2 teaspoons grated orange zest

salt -- to taste

Here are all the colors of a brilliant autumn day. Since sweet potatoes cook more quickly than beets, cut them into thicker slices, which are more likely to keep their shape. The beet greens add a very appealing spinach-like flavor. The pressure cooker tenderized beet skins so much that removing them becomes more a matter of aesthetics than necessity.

Cut the beets from their greens and peel or scrub them. Cut the beets into 1/4 -inch slices and cut the slices in half. Set aside.

Cut and discard the red stems from the beet greens. Rinse the beet green in a sinkful of cold water, taking care to remove all of the sand. Discard any blemished or very large, tough leaves. Drain and chop the beet greens into strips about 2 inches wide. Use about 4 cups of tightly packed chopped greens for the soup, saving the remainder for stock or another use. (They're delicious if you saute in olive oil with lots of garlic).

Cut the peeled sweet potatoes into 1/2-inch slices and cut the slices in half. Set aside. Heat the butter in the cooker. Add 2 teaspoons of the ginger and the onions and cook until the onions are soft, about 3 minutes. add the beet greens, sliced beets, sweet potatoes, and stock.

Lock the lid in place and over high heat bring to high pressure. adjust the heat to maintain high pressure, and cook for 7 minutes. Reduce the pressure with a quick-release method. Remove the lid, tilting it away from you to allow any excess steam to escape. Stir in the remaining 1/4 teaspoon ginger and the orange zest. Add salt to taste and serve immediately.

Bunch of Beets & Friend Cabbage Borsch

1 Med Cabbage -- sliced or wedge
3 Garlic -- cloves minced
4 Medium Beets
3 Carrot s
1 Lrg Onion
2 Celery -- stalks cut in 3rds
3 lbs meat/marrow bones
2 Fresh Lemons
2 cans (19 oz.) whole Tomatoes -- do not drain

This is a hearty sweet and sour meat soup that can be used as a main dish. Measurements were never exact. You need to taste. Put meat and bones in a 8 or 12 qt stock pot. Put in cans of tomato, cover with water and bring to a boil. In the meantime, get the veggies ready. Slice beets and carrots, others go in whole. When stock boils, skim off top foam. Put in beets, carrots, garlic, and other veggies. Turn heat down to a simmer for about an hour, keep lid on askew. Add garlic and sugar.

SPLENDA has been used. Amounts are a matter of preference. It should have a rich, sweet and sour taste. Break up any meat chunks and stir it back into the soup before serving.

Doukabor Vegetable Soup

This soup was created originally by Russian emigrants who settled in Canada. They wanted a soup of the same nature as borscht that would be hearty and warm. Normally a dairy soup; this version is vegan.

1 medium-sized raw beet unpeeled, or 1 16-ounce can whole beets

1 large unpeeled potato, julienned

1 medium carrot, peeled and diced

1/2 large onion, diced

1 small wedge (1/2-inch) green cabbage, shredded

1/3 of a medium green bell pepper, seeded and diced

2 tablespoons oil

1/3 cup tomato paste mixed with 1/3 cup water

1- 1/2 to 2 cups water

1 teaspoon dill weed

1 1/2 teaspoons minced garlic

1 teaspoon sea salt

3/4 teaspoon ground caraway seeds

Sour Cream

Chopped fresh dill, for garnish

Cut the unpeeled beet into julienned pieces. If you are using canned beets, drain, reserve the liquid, and set aside three of the beets for another use. Cut the remaining beets into julienned pieces. Measure the juice, add water to make 2 1/2 cups, and set aside for the soup.

Saute the vegetables in the oil for about 5 minutes over medium heat. Add the tomato paste mixture and the water (or beet juice and water mixture). Add and stir in the dill weed, garlic, salt, and ground caraway seed. Cover and simmer for about 30 minutes.

Serve the soup hot. Add a small dollop of <u>Sour Cream</u> to each small bowl. Garnish with fresh dill. (As an alternative, you could stir the sour cream with 1 Tbsp of potato flakes for thickening into the soup before serving; use 3 tablespoons for the entire recipe of soup.)

Angie's Beet Soup

1 onion
8 medium red beets
4 parsnips
5-6 carrots
1-2 zucchini or other squash
2 cups cauliflower
2 peeled potatoes diced
1 can of veg stock (or water with veg bouillon, if you prefer)
2 cups cooked white cannelloni or garbanzos beans

In a big stock pot, saute the onions and carrots in olive oil. Gradually add other vegetables - parsnips, zucchini, etc. When it seems to need liquid, add the veg stock. Then add water as needed. You can vary the saltiness by adding more water. Keep adding veggies and water until everything is in the pot, and it's bubbling away.

Cook it all up for an hour or so, or until the veggies are pretty soft. I like to cook soups on a lower heat for a longer time, if possible develop flavors. Blend all ingredients (you will have to do this in shifts.)Serve with cream and/or green onions to garnish.

Boris Beet Soup

1 cup dried Navy beans	8 Med. Beets
2- 1/2 lb lean beef	2 cup red cabbage, shredded
1/2 lb slab bacon	2 large leeks, sliced
10 cup cold water	3 medium potatoes, in a 1 inch dice
1 bay leaf	1 canned (13 oz) whole tomato
8 whole peppercorns	1 tbsp . Tomato paste
2 cloves garlic	3 tbsp Red wine vinegar
2 tbsp Dried parsley	4 tbsp Sugar
1 Carrot	1 lb Kielbasa (opt)
1 Celery stalk	2 tbsp Flour
1 Large red onion	1 tbsp Butter, melted
Salt to taste	1/2 cup Sour cream

Cover beans with water and allow to soak overnight; cook until tender; drain; set aside. Place beef, bacon and water in large soup pot; bring to a boil. Skim fat from surface. Add bay leaf, peppercorns, garlic, parsley, carrot, celery, onion and salt.

Cover and simmer over low heat for about 1 1/2 hours. Scrub beets for soup and cook in boiling water until tender, about 45 minutes; drain and discard water; cool. Peel and cut each beet into eighths. Scrub 8 small beets; grate; cover with water to soak.

Remove meat from soup; set aside. Strain soup into another pot and add cooked beets, cabbage, leeks, potatoes, tomatoes, tomato paste, vinegar, sugar, beef and bacon. Bring to a boil and simmer 45 minutes.

Cut kielbasa into chunks and add with navy beans to soup. Simmer 20 minutes more. Mix flour and butter together to form paste. Stir into soup to thicken slightly. Strain raw beets, saving liquid and discard beets. Add beet liquid to soup.

Additional sugar or vinegar may be added for sweeter or more sour flavor. Slice meat and arrange in individual soup bowls. Pour hot soup with vegetables over meat. Garnish each serving with a dollop of sour cream, if desired.

French Beet & Beaujolias Borscht

4 medium beets, peeled and diced
1 ½ small red onion, chopped
1 medium pear, peeled, cored and diced
1-1/2 Tbsp. raw white rice
2-1/4 cups of water
1-1/2 Tbsp of sugar
1 cup Beaujolais nouveau wine
1-1/2 Tbsp . raspberry vinegar
1 teaspoon finely grated lemon rind
salt and pepper
Sour Cream to garnish

Put the beets, onion, pear and rice in a sauce pan. Add the water and heat to boiling over high heat. Reduce heat and simmer uncovered for about 30 minutes. The beets should be very tender. Stir in the sugar, vinegar, and wine. Working in butches, puee the soup in a blender. Season with salt and pepper. Strain the soup through a fine sieve. Stir in lemon zest.
To Serve: Can be served hot or cold. Garnish with a bit of sour cream

Beautiful Beet Soup....... To Die For, Oy!

8 medium beets

2 turnips, peeled

1 potato

2 carrots

2 cups shredded cabbage

2 cups chopped onion

2 tablespoons margarine or butter

1 teaspoon caraway seeds

2 to 3 quarts stock or water

1 teaspoon dried dill, or 2 tablespoons fresh

1/2 cup cider vinegar

1 tablespoon honey

1 cup tomato puree

1/2 cup orange juice

1/4 teaspoon paprika

salt, to taste

sour cream or fresh dill sprigs, for garnish

SCRUB THE beets, trim the ends, and grate. Chop or slice the turnips, potato, and carrots. Beets can be messy to prepare, so grate them last (and don't wear white!). In a large stock pot, saue the onion in margarine or butter for a few minutes, then add the caraway and the rest of the vegetables. Add the stock and the remaining ingredients. If you use fresh dill, add it at the end. Cover and simmer for 40 to 45 minutes, testing occasionally for doneness. Once cooked, you can puree this soup in a blender or food processor for a more delicate texture. Serve hot, garnished with a dollop of sour cream or a sprig of dill. *Serves 8.*

Lithuanian Beet Farmer Borsch

1 Bunch of beets Peeled, halved, sliced

1 cup Beet greens, Washed and finely chopped

3 stalks celery, diced

1 Tbsp. Lemon juice

Salt & pepper to taste

1 large onion, diced

4 Carrots, sliced

1 Tbsp. Vinegar

1 Tbsp. Horseradish

1 can Tomato soup

Put vegetables in a large pot with water to cover. Add remaining ingredients and mix thoroughly. Simmer 2 - 2 1/2 hours, until beets and carrots are tender

Cream of Beet Soup
(For a Large Gathering)

In a 20 qt. pot:
5 qt. water
1- 1/2 lb. diced onion
1- 1/2 lb. diced carrot
1- 1/2 lb. diced celery

Bring to the boil and **add 12 lb. shredded beets** (undrained), **3 lb. canned tomatoes** (peeled and crushed), 4 oz. white vinegar, 3/4 c. sugar, 4 Tbsp. salt, 3 Tbsp. garlic powder, 1 Tbsp. white pepper and 1/2 lb. beef broth base. Simmer for 1 hour. Mix 4 cup. flour and 2 1/2 lb. sour cream with about 2 qt. cold milk to the consistency of a milkshake. Add some of the hot liquid (temper the sour cream mixture) and mix into the soup to thicken. Heat through. (makes 80 (8 oz.) servings)

Cream of Beet Soup for Your Home

In a 4 qt. pot: place
1 pint (16 oz.) water
1/3 cup diced onion
1/3 cup diced carrot
1/3 cup diced celery

Bring to the boil. Add 1 **can (20 oz.) shredded beets (undrained)**, **1 can (5 oz.) canned whole tomatoe**s (peeled and crushed), 2 tbsp. white vinegar, 2 tsp. red food color, 1 rounded Tbsp. sugar, 1 rounded tbsp. salt (or to taste), 1 scant tsp. garlic powder (or to taste), rounded 1/3 tsp. white pepper and 1 oz. beef base. Simmer 1 hour. Mix a scant 1/2 cup. flour and a scant 1/2 cup. sour cream with about 3/4 cup cold milk to make the consistency of a milkshake. Stir in some of the hot liquid and return to the pot to thicken the soup. Heat through. (serves 10-12)

Cold Beet Soup

1 can (15 oz) beets
2 tablespoons lemon juice
2 teaspoons sugar
1/4 cup minced onion
water
1 1/4 cup sour cream

Drain the liquid from the can of beets. Put in a measuring cup and add water to make one cup. Place lemon juice, onion, sugar and beets plus liquid into a blender and puree until mixture is smooth.

Pour into a plastic covered container (I use a long flat one) and place in the freezer. After a while ice crystals will form around the edges. When there is quite a rim of ice, remove from the freezer and stir well. Either stir cold sour cream into the soup until it makes a nice pink color or pour the soup into a dish and serve with a dollop of sour cream on top.

This is better with fresh cooked beets but so easy with the canned beets! Yummmm!

Beet Soup with Dill and Yogurt

1 Tbs. Oil

1 med. Onion; sliced

3 cups Beets peeled and coarsely diced,

1 qt Chicken stock; or canned- low-sodium chicken broth

1 tsp Salt

3/4 cup Plain yogurt

3 Tbsp Chopped fresh dill

Heat oil in a Dutch oven over low heat. Add onions and cook, stirring, about 12 minutes. Add beets and cook, covered, about 35 minutes, stirring occasionally, until beets are falling apart. Add stock and salt. Cover and bring to boil. Reduce heat and simmer 15 minutes. Strain and reserve liquid. Transfer beets to blender or food processor and puree until smooth. Return puree to pot and add reserved liquid. Pour hot soup into tureen and ladle soup into bowls in front of guests. Decorate each soup bowl with 2 tablespoons yogurt and sprinkle yogurt with chopped dill.

Italian Borscht

Minestra di pane is one of the best uses for sliced Tuscan bread (crusty, firm of crumb, and without salt) I have ever come across. Tuscans make this hearty winter soup with *cavolo nero,* a long-leafed variety of winter cabbage whose leaves are a very dark purplish green. If you cannot find *cavolo nero,* use the tender small leaves of black-leaf kale. To serve six you will need:

1 pound dried white beans, washed and soaked for three hours

A small onion, a small carrot, a six inch stick of celery, and a small bunch of parsley, minced together

1/4 cup olive oil

1 1/2 tablespoons tomato paste

1/2 pound *cavolo nero* or black-leaf kale, shredded

1 pound beet greens, ribbed and shredded

1/2 pound potatoes, peeled and diced

Salt, pepper, and a sprig of thyme

Thinly sliced day old Italian or French white bread

Olive oil (to be used at the table)

Boil the beans in lightly salted water. When they're almost cooked, saute the onion mixture in the oil, in a heavy bottomed pot. When the onion has become translucent, add the tomato paste and the liquid from the beans. Add the cabbage, beet greens, and potatoes. Stir in the beans and season to taste with salt, pepper, and a sprig of thyme. Simmer until the potatoes are cooked (taste a piece for doneness), and remove the thyme. Take an ovenproof serving dish and fill it with alternating layers of thinly sliced bread and soup, making sure the bread is damp, until the soup is used up.

Served immediately, this dish is called *minestra di pane,* or bread soup. However, it improves dramatically with age, so much that when it is reheated and served the next day it is called *ribollita,* reboiled, and is one of the few reasons to get excited about the arrival of winter. Serve it as a first course, with a cruet of extra virgin olive oil so your diners can sprinkle it into their soup according to their taste. The wine? A light zesty red, for example a Chianti Putto would go well.

Baby Beet Borsch

1 lb can shoestring beets
2 cans water
1/2 cup sugar
1/2 cup bottled lemon juice
2 tsp. salt
Sour cream
Cucumber slices, optional

In 2 quart saucepan, combine beets, water, sugar, lemon juice and salt. Heat to boiling. Lower heat and simmer for about 2 minutes.
Chill thoroughly. When ready to serve, top with dolup sour cream and cucumber slices. Yield: 4 to 6 servings.

Borsch with Meat

Some like to simmer the beef and bacon for up to 6 hours, then let sit overnight in the broth to cool. Skim the excess fat and cut the meats into bite-size pieces. Reheat, adding the beets, cabbage, onions, leeks, and sausage. I don't think that the carrots are necessary or add anything to the recipe. I've added several varieties of sausage to give added flavors but the milder Polish sausages seem to go better with the soft and sweet flavors of the beets. Serve with fresh bread. Prep Time: approx. 30 Minutes. Cook Time: approx. 2 Hours 10 Minutes. Ready in: approx. 10 Hours 40 Minutes. Makes 12 servings.

1 1/2 pounds beets, boiled and grated

2 tablespoons red wine vinegar

1 teaspoon white sugar

1 pound lean beef chuck

2 quarts water

1/2 pound bacon

1 tablespoon salt

8 whole black peppercorns

6 sprigs of fresh parsley

2 teaspoons dried marjoram

2 teaspoons dill seed

1 pound shredded cabbage

2 leeks, sliced

1 cup chopped onion

1 carrot, grated

2 pounds Polish sausage

2 tablespoons chopped fresh dill weed

Combine 1/2 cup of the beets, the vinegar, and sugar in a small bowl; refrigerate, covered, overnight. Refrigerate remaining beets. Place beef, water, bacon, salt, peppercorns, parsley sprigs, marjoram, and dill seeds (or basil leaves) in Dutch oven. Heat to boiling. Reduce heat, simmer, partially covered, over medium heat until beef is tender (about 2 hours). Discard parsley sprigs. Add 3 cups beets, the cabbage, leeks, onions, carrot, and sausage; simmer, covered, over low heat 30 minutes. To serve, remove beef, bacon, and sausage; cut into 2-inch pieces. Return meats and reserved beet mixture to Dutch oven. Sprinkle with snipped dill. Pass with sour cream.

Beef Borsch

3 lbs beef shank
1 lb boneless beef brisket
2 qts. water
1 Tbsp salt
1/4 tsp. pepper
4 cups shredded cabbage
2 cups onion, chopped
28 oz can tomatoes, cut up
1/4 cup lemon juice
1/4 cup snipped parsley
3 Tbsp. sugar
2 cloves garlic, minced
1 tsp paprika
1 bay leaf
16 oz can beets, diced
sour cream

Simmer meat, water, salt and pepper 2 hours, covered. Remove bones.
Dice meat and return to broth. Add remaining ingredients to the broth except
the beets and sour cream. Cover and simmer one hour. Add beets, heat through.
Remove bay leaf. Season to taste. Top each serving with a dollop of sour cream.
Serves 12-14.

Innisfree Borsch

1 lb. stewing beef

2 average red beets

2 cups cabbage shredded

4 little potatoes

1 carrot

2 tomatoes

1 tsp. vinegar

salt and pepper, to taste

parsley

dill

spring onions

Borsch is soup, but it is 'Borscht', no one calls it soup in Russia. History says that Borsch was and is one of the most popular dishes in Russia. It appeared at the end of the 18th and 19th centuries. The main ingredients are red beets and broths made from meat or fish, mushrooms, or smoked sausages. Plus, people used to and do use cabbage, onions, carrots, potatoes, tomatoes, spinach, and sorrel. The sour taste it can have is because of the vinegar. Our ancestry ate borsch with pancakes, different porridges, and pies. Poor people made borsch without any meat, only with vegetables.

Preparing meat broth-

Put beef into a large saucepan and cover with 3 liters cold water. Bring to a boil and reduce heat. Remove the grease froth from the broth surface with a spoon. Add one onion. Cook at low heat for 1-2 hours.

Simmering Red Beets-

Melt 1 Tbs. margarine in a saucepan. Cut red beets into thin sticks and add them into the cooking pot. Add tomato paste or sliced tomatoes. Simmer at low heat for 1 hour. If there is not enough liquid, add some broth. Add vinegar.

Pan-frying Vegetables-

Melt 1 Tbs. margarine in a frying pan. Add chopped onions and carrots that are cut into thin sticks. Cover and saute for 15 minutes, stirring occasionally.

Heat broth to boiling. Add chopped cabbage and potatoes that are cut into bars. Cook for 5 minutes. Add saute and cook another 10 minutes. Add simmered red beets. Cook another 5 minutes. Add salt and black pepper. If you like garlic, you can add about 5g grated garlic. It is supposed to be in borsch. I don't like it and never add it here. Borsch is served with sour cream.

Vegreville Borsch

1c Navy beans, dry

2 -1/2 lb. Lean beef

1/2 lb Slab bacon

10 cup Cold water

1 Bay leaf

8 Whole peppercorns

2 Cloves garlic

2 tbsp Dried parsley

1 Carrot

1 Celery stalk

1 lrg Red onion

1 tsp Salt (opt)

8 Beets for soup

2 cup green cabbage, shredded

2 lg Leeks, sliced

3 md Potatoes, diced

1 can (28 oz.)tomatoes

1 Tbsp Tomato paste

3 Tbsp Red wine vinegar

4 Tbsp Sugar

1 lb Kielbasa (opt)

2 Tbsp Flour

1 Tbsp melted butter

1/2 cup Sour cream

Cover beans with water and allow to soak overnight; cook until tender;drain; set aside. Place beef, bacon and water in large soup pot; bring to a boil. Skim fat from surface. Add bay leaf, peppercorns, garlic,parsley, carrot, celery, onion and salt. Cover and simmer over low heat for about 1 1/2 hours. Scrub beets and cook in boiling water until tender, about 45 minutes; drain and discard water; cool. Peel and dice each beet 1/2 inch size or grate. Remove meat from soup pot; set aside. Strain liquid into another pot and add cooked beets, cabbage, leeks, potatoes, tomatoes, tomato paste, vinegar,sugar, beef and bacon. Bring to a boil and simmer 45 minutes. Cut kielbasa into chunks and add with navy beans to soup. Simmer 20 minutes more. Mix flour and butter together to form paste. Stir into soup to thicken slightly. Additional sugar or vinegar may be added for sweeter or more sour flavor.Slice meat and arrange in individual soup bowls. Pour hot soup with vegetables over meat. Garnish each serving with a dollop of sour cream, if desired. Serves 10

Chilled Sweet & Sour Borsch

3 medium-sized beets (and tender tops if you like)
1 Small onion chopped
1 lb. bulk sausage -- crumbled
2 Large carrots diced
2 cups red or green cabbage shredded
1/4 cup lemon juice
2 Tbsp. sugar
1/4 tsp. dill weed
6 cup chicken stock

Saute the onion and sausage; drain off grease. Add the beets, carrots, cabbage, lemon juice, sugar, chicken stock (stock can be made with 2 teaspoons chicken bouillon or cubes and 6 cups water). Cover; bring to a boil, then reduce heat. Simmer for 45 minutes. Serve with a dollop of sour cream or yogurt and dill weed.

Note: You can leave out the sausage; Season with spices of choice. Chill and blend with some sour cream in a blender and serve as a chilled soup. Garnish with a dollop of sour cream or yogurt and dill weed.

Pisnyi Borsch (Meatless Beet Soup)

2 lb. Beets

1 lrg. Carrot

1 med. Parsnip

1 med. Turnip

2 lrg. Celery Ribs

2 med. Onions

1 lrg. Bay Leaf

3 -4 whole Peppercorns

3 Dried Boletus OR 1/2 lb Chopped
Mushrooms of choice

1 qt. Beet Kvas* **OR**

1 tsp Sour Salt Crystalized

-Citric Acid If Not Using-Kvas*

(*Sauerkraut juice)

2 tsp. Salt

1 tsp. Ground Pepper

2 tsp. Fresh Dill weed Chopped

Soak Boletus overnight. Cook in a little water until tender. Cool, reserving the liquid, and chop finely. Scrub the beets and cut into quarters. Cover with water and cook over low heat until tender, about 1 to 2 hours. Cool and pour off the liquid, reserving it. Slip off the peels. (Wear rubber gloves to prevent purple hands.) This may be done a day in advance.

Peel and cut up the other vegetables. Add the bay leaf, peppercorns, and boletus or mushrooms to the vegetables, with enough water to cover, and cook, in a large aluminum pot over low heat, until tender. Strain the beet liquid into the vegetables. Shred the beets in a processor or on a medium grater, and add. Simmer for about 10 minutes and strain into a large pot. To keep the broth clear, do not press the vegetables. Add the beet kvas, mushroom liquid, pepper and salt. Bring to a gentle boil, then turn the heat low. Taste, the flavor should be tart, mellow, and full. For more tartness, add fresh lemon juice or sour salt. Keeps well in the refrigerator. Reheat gently; do not overcook or the color will turn brown. To serve, pour over 3 or 4 vushka (dumplings) in soup plates and garnish with the fresh dill.

Mundare Winter Borsch

1 cup barley

1/2 cup mixed baby lima beans, split peas, brown lentils

1 tbs. olive oil

6 cups water

2 tbs. miso

1 large onion, chopped

5-6 turnips, peeled and cubed (or 2 parsnips, or 2 potatoes)

2 carrots, sliced about 1/2" thick

1/2-3/4 pound mushrooms, sliced

3 cloves garlic, minced

1/2 tsp pepper (or to taste)

2 tsp marjoram

1 tsp rosemary

1/3 cup tamari

3 tbs. margerine

Saute the garlic and onion in olive oil on medium heat until the onions are translucent. Combine the barley, lima beans, split peas, lentils, miso, and water with the onion/garlic, and bring to a boil. Add the turnips and carrots, reduce heat to medium-low, and simmer for about 1 1/2 hours, stirring occasionally. ("But grandma, where did they get miso in the Ukraine?" "Shut up and eat your soup.") If you have broccoli stems, peel and slice them and add them at this point. you also snagged about 1 cup of shredded/sliced cabbage from the main dish, and added about 1/2 hour before the soup was done. Add the mushrooms, spices and tamari and continue cooking on a low heat for another hour. Add the margarine, let sit for a few minutes, and serve. If cooking the night before, you might want to add 1 cup of water and heat again just before serving; the barley tends to absorb water, and if you omit this extra water you end up with a tasty gruel.

Odessa Borsch

10 beets peeled and julienne
5 onions thinly sliced
3 carrots peeled and shredded
Med head red or green cabbage shredded
4 cups chopped beet greens
1/4 cup cider vinegar or brown rice vinegar
salt, if desired

Slice the veggies, put them into a large soup pot and fill with water to about 1 -1/2 to 2 inches above the vegetables. Add salt to taste.

Bring to a boil, then reduce heat. Simmer as long as possible over the lowest heat possible. When the vegetables are soft, mash them with a potato masher (do not put into a blender or food processor; the idea is to have a coarse soup, not a cream soup). Add vinegar to taste.

Continue to simmer; you want all the flavors to blend.

Serve with a kasha dish and Russian black bread.

A great cold-weather meal; this is the best borsch recipe **this s**ide *of Odessa . There are others on the* **other** *side of Odessa. ;-)*

Borsch for the Soul

Finely shred:
1/2 head small green cabbage
4 peeled beets
1 onion
1 carrot

Heat a little oil in frying pan, add 1 bay leaf, a few whole cloves, and several peppercorns.
Add the vegetables and saute a few minutes.
Transfer to cooking pot and add equal amounts of tomato juice and apple cider to cover the vegetables. Simmer 30-40 minutes.
Now add lemon juice or vinegar until the broth is distinctly tart, balanced by the sweetness of the cider.
Add salt to taste.
Serve with shredded horseradish.

Ethnic Mama Borscht

5 lb. beets with the tops enough water to cover the beets at least 3 to 4 times
their height
2-3 large onions
3 tablespoons salt
1/4 to 1/2 cup lemon juice
1/4 cup honey (optional)

Cut off beet greens from the beets but leave about an inch or two of the stocks
on top of the beets. **SCRUB** the beets thoroughly. SCRUB the beets thoroughly
and when you think you are done, do it again for good measure! In a **LARGE**
pot (the likelihood of the borsch boiling over and you dying your clothes red is
minimized if you use a pot that is larger than the beets and liquid combined-
-it is less messy to cook a small amount in a large pot than a large amount in
a small pot. It also impresses your husband (wife) and friends as it gives them
the idea that you take your cooking seriously. OK back to the recipe...
Put the beets in a large pot. Cover them with water. Make sure it is COLD
water. Bring the water to a boil. Boil about 15-25 minutes until the beets are
tender . Remove the beets from the water. Pop the skins off the beets. **DO NOT
THROW OUT THE WATER!** This is the beet juice !!!!!!!! Strain the beet juice
through a cheesecloth sieve. Peel the onion. Hint: The easiest way to peel an
onion is to cut the onion in quarters. With the tip of the onion on the cutting
board, take your knife and cut off a tiny portion off the tip on both ends, The
onion peels slide off easily and you can use these onion peels in your chicken
soup base! Grate the beets. Grate the onion. (Use a food processor and your
eyes won't tear and your knuckles will be intact.) Wearing clean rubber gloves
for this step is allowed
Put the grated onion and beets into the pot with the **STRAINED** beet juice.
You can add the beet tops, which you have chopped into nice tiny little pieces.
Bring to a quick boil. Add the salt, lemon juice and honey and simmer until the
honey has dissolved. Serve this borscht hot with a potato and dill sprigs in the
center. It can also be served chilled as cool soup on a hot day!

Lavoy Borscht

2 small onions
2 small carrots
Few parsley stalks
1 bay leaf
1 pound raw beet root
salt
pepper
2 pints chicken stock
Juice of 1/2 lemon
5 oz. carton sour cream

Peel and finely chop the onions and carrots and put them in a saucepan with the parsley stalks and bay leaf. Peel and grate the beet root, add to the pan, season with salt and pepper and pour in the chicken stock. Bring to the boil and simmer for 30 minutes. Strain the soup if you prefer it clear. Add lemon juice and check seasoning. Serve in bowls garnished with the sour cream. Serves 6.

Polish Borsch

1 1/2 pounds beef chuck, cut up
1 1/2 quarts water
4 medium beets, cooked and sliced
2 celery stalks, diced
1 onion, minced
salt and pepper
1/4 cup dairy sour cream
2 tablespoons all-purpose flour
1 egg

Put meat in kettle and add water. Bring to boil and simmer, covered, for 1 1/2 - 2 hours, or until meat is almost tender. add beets, celery, and onion, Cook for about 30 minutes longer. Season to taste. Blend sour cream, flour and egg. Stir into soup, bring again to boil. Serve in soup bowls and pass boiled potatoes.

Pork Fat Borsch

2 medium beets
5 medium potatoes
1 small head cabbage
1 onion
2 middle carrots
1/4 lb. of meat (FAT pork)
1 teaspoon vinegar
1 teaspoon sugar
2 Tbsp Butter

Take beets. Don't peel or cut. Boil till half done . Remove from water and set aside to cool.Make strong meat bouillon. Boil meat about 1.5 hours.
Cut potatoes into small cubes, put into bouillon, simmer on low heat, so water do not boil. Cut and add carrots. Cut and add cabbage. Add grated beets. Add vinegar, sugar and salt to your own taste. Saute onion in butter till it takes on a golden color. Add into borscht about 5 minutes before ready. Serve with sour cream and garlic bread.

Winter Borsch

4 lbs beets, large

6 cups water

4 Tbsp. red wine vinegar (4-6)

3 Tbsp. salad oil

2 onions, large chopped

3 carrots, finely chopped

1 yellow or red bell pepper, seeded, finely chop

3 Roma tomato, cored, chopped

3 qts. beef broth (3.5 if using meat)

4 lbs beef shanks (optional)

4 russet potatoes, large cubed to 1/2"

1 head of cabbage, small cored, finely chop

1/3 c fresh basil (or 2 Tbsp. dry) chopped

4 cloves garlic minced

salt to taste

2 Tbsp. sugar (2-3)

2 Tbsp. parsley chopped

1 cup sour cream (optional)

1/3 c fresh dill (or 2 Tbsp. dry) (optional) chopped

lemon wedges (optional)

dried red chili peppers (optional)

2 stalks celery quartered

4 sprigs fresh dill (or 1/2 tsp dry)

3 sprigs fresh parsley

1 bay leaf

8 black peppercorns

8 whole allspice

1 dried red chili pepper

Tie together celery, dill, parsley, bay, peppercorns, allspice and chili pepper in cheesecloth for bouquet garni.

Trim tops off beets, scrub and rinse well. Cook covered in water plus 1/4 c vinegar until tender, about 45 min.. Remove from liquid (save), cool, remove skin, stems and roots, and slice into small (1/4") sticks. In large (12 qt.) pot saute onion in oil over med-high heat w/stirring until limp (~5 min.). Add carrots and bell pepper and saute about 10 min. until lightly browned. Add tomatoes and cook about 2' until soft. Add broth, bouquet garni and meat. Bring to boil and cook covered until meat is tender (~2 hours).

Remove meat, cool, remove fat and bones and break into bite-sized pieces.

Add potatoes; cover and cook until tender. Add cabbage; cover and cook until limp (~10 min.). Discard seasoning packet. Add beets and cooking liquid, meat and basil. Bring to boil, add garlic, salt, sugar and 1-2 Tbsp.. vinegar. If made ahead, cool, cover and chill. Reheat to serve. Sprinkle w/parsley in individual bowls. Serve with sour cream, dill, lemon, and chili's.

Spare Rib Borsch

1 lb spare ribs, cut short
1-1/2 onions, chopped
3 large carrots, diced
2 large potatoes, peeled & cubed
3-5 cups beets, cooked & shredded
1 cup peas
2 tsp salt
1/2 tsp pepper
2 Tbsp vinegar
1 tsp dry dill weed

Cover spare ribs in pot . Bring to a boil. Lower heat Cover & simmer for about 1 hour. Skim off any foam which comes to the top. Add remainder of ingredients. Simmer until vegetables are cooked. Use whipping or sour cream if desired for final flavor finish.

Sweet & Sour Borsch II

3 medium size beets with leafy tops
2 Tbsp. salad oil
1 small onion, chopped
2 large carrots, diced
2 cups coarsely shredded red or green cabbage
1/4 cup lemon juice
2 -1/2 Tbsp. sugar
1/2 tsp. dill weed
6 cups vegetable stock
salt and pepper

Cut off beet tops. Cut off and discard stems and wilted leaves.
Coarsely chop remaining leaves. Peed beets and shred coarsely; set aside.
Heat oil in a 5 qt pan over medium heat. Add onion and carrot and cook, stirring occasionally until vegetables are soft (about 10 minutes). Add beets and tops, cabbage, lemon juice, sugar, dill and stock; bring to simmering. Reduce heat to low; cover and simmer until beets and cabbage are tender (about 45 minutes). Season with salt and pepper to taste. Serve with a dollop of sour cream.

Party Borsch

(Serves 15)
3 beets, Approx. 3 inch diameter, peeled & cut into thin strips
1 carrot, diced
8 cups water
1 medium potato, diced
2 Tbsp lemon juice
1/2 cup string beans or green peas
1 large onion, sliced
1 Tbsp butter (optional)
1 -1/2 cup cabbage, shredded
1 cup tomato juice (or tomato soup)
1- 1/2 tsp flour
1/2 cup water, cold
2 Tbsp fresh dill, chopped
salt and pepper to taste

Cook beets and carrots in water for 20 minutes. Add potatoes, simmer for 10-15 minutes. Add lemon juice, beans or peas and simmer until tender. Steam fry or saute onion in margarine or butter until soft.

Add cabbage to onion with 1/4 cup water, simmer until cabbage is tender. Stir into the beets. Add tomato juice or soup and salt and pepper to taste. Blend flour with 1/2 cup cold water, stir into vegetables. Add dill and bring to boil for 5-10 minutes. Serve hot.

Borsch of the Karpatas
(Karpathain Mountains)

1 cup cabbage, finely chopped
1 cup potatoes, diced
1/2 cup carrots, diced
1 stick celery, minced
1 small onion, chopped
2 quarts stock
3 Tbsp. butter
1 1/2 cups tomatoes, peeled and seeded
1/2 cup beet juice
1 cup beets, diced and cooked
1 tsp. vinegar
salt and pepper
1 pint sour cream
parsley, finely chopped

Prepare vegetables. Heat the stock to boiling.

In a heavy pan melt the butter. Turn the heat to low and put the vegetables into the pan, cover and simmer for 5 minutes shaking the pan from time to time. Add the hot stock. Put the tomatoes into a food processor and make a fine puree. Add this to the soup. Add the beet juice and simmer gently. When the vegetables are tender add beets and vinegar. Season with the salt and pepper to taste.

Remove from the heat before the beets lose their color. Serve with a tsp. of sour cream and a little parsley on each portion.

Chicken ? Borscht *Sure!*

Yields 1 gallon
2 pounds whole beets
1 gallon Chicken Stock
4 oz leeks, julienned
3 oz cabbage, julienned
3 oz onions, julienned
3 oz celery, julienned
sachet of parsley, black peppercorns, bay leaf, thyme and fennel
beef brisket, cooked, julienned
red wine vinegar
creme fraiche
fresh dill

Cook the beets in half of the stock until tender, drain and reserve the liquid. Sweat the remaining vegetables until the onions are translucent. Add the remaining stock and sachet and simmer the vegetables until tender. Peel the cooked beets and julienne. Add the beets and reserved cooking liquid to the simmering vegetables. Degrease the soup. Add the beef. Add the vinegar and adjust the seasoning with kosher salt and freshly ground pepper. Garnish each serving with the creme fraiche and dill sprig.

Ukrainian Borscht

1 onion, chopped
2 cloves garlic, peeled and finely chopped
2 tbsp. butter
1/2 large celeriac, peeled and coarsely grated
1 large parsnip, peeled and coarsely grated
3 cups raw beet root, peeled and coarsely grated
4 tomatoes, skinned, seeded and roughly chopped
1/2 teaspoon sugar, up to 1 tsp.
3 Tbsp red wine vinegar, (3 to 5)
8 cups rich beef stock
salt and ground black pepper
2 cups potatoes, peeled and cut into chunks
1/2 large green cabbage, cored and shredded

In a large saucepan cook the onion and garlic gently in the butter, without browning, until tender. Add the celeriac, parsnip, beet root and half the tomatoes. Mix in the sugar, 3 Tbsp of vinegar, 300 ml stock, salt and pepper. Stir and bring to the boil, then cover and leave to simmer for 40 minutes. Meanwhile, pour the remaining stock into another large saucepan
and bring to the boil. Add the potatoes and cabbage and simmer, half- covered, for 15-20 minutes until the potatoes are tender. When both pans of vegetables are ready combine them in the largest pan, adding the rest of the tomatoes. Bring back to the boil, simmer for 5-10 minutes, then taste and add a little more seasoning, sugar or vinegar as necessary.
Serve in deep soup bowls, topping each bowlful with a dollop of sour cream and a sprinkling of chopped parsley.

Cole Slaw Borsch

2 cups shredded cabbage (or 2 cups packaged cole slaw mix)
1 cup chopped onion
1 stalk chopped celery
2 Tbsp butter
15 oz can julienned beets, undrained
8 oz can tomato sauce
1 Tbsp brown sugar
1 bay leaf
pinch rosemary
2 Tbsp lemon juice
3 hard boiled eggs peeled and diced

Saute cabbage, onion and celery in butter until soft in large saucepan. Add tomato sauce, beets with juice, herbs, sugar and enough water to cover ingredients. Bring to boil, reduce heat, simmer 25-30 minutes. Add lemon juice a few minutes before serving.

Serve garnished with chopped boiled eggs, sour cream and pumpernickel bread.

Tomato Soup Borsch

6 to 8 beets
8 cups water
1 tsp. fresh dill
1 can Cream of Tomato soup
sour cream

Scrub well beets (do not peel them). Put in large pot with 8 cups water. Bring to boil and then reduce to simmer and cook until tender. (Save cooking beet water). When tender take slotted spoon and put beets immediately into cold water. Slip skins off with your hands. If you have a Cuisinart, chop beets into tiny pieces. If no Cuisinart, then you will have to chop the beets up by hand. Put chopped beets into pot, add fresh dill, chopped, 1 can Tomato soup (undiluted) and 6 cups of the cooking beet water. If you want a thinner borscht use a little more of the beet water.

Stir well. Serve with 1 Tbsp. sour cream per individual serving.

Add salt to your own taste.

Noble Borsch (Garlic Beet Soup)

3 quarts water
2 pounds flank steak or brisket beef bones
8 beets, grated
2 onions, diced
2 cloves garlic, minced
1 tbs. salt
3 tbs. brown sugar
sour salt or lemon juice to taste
2 eggs, beaten (optional)

In a deep saucepan, combine the water, meat and bones. Bring to a boil and skim. Add the beets, onions, garlic and salt. Cover and cook over medium heat for 2 hours. Add the brown sugar and sour salt or lemon juice. Cook 30 minutes longer. Taste and adjust the seasoning.
If using the eggs, beat them in a small bowl. Gradually add a little hot soup, beating steadily to prevent curdling. Add the egg liquid to the saucepan, beating it in very well. Serve

Borschti Ukraininskii

1 quart water	1 large carrot, scraped, diced
2 quarts beef stock	1 onion, med. coarse chopped
3 Tbsp sunflower oil	1 cabbage head small shredded
2 cup beer	3 Tbsp. tomato paste
2 beets, large peeled and julienned	1- 1/2 Tbsp. salt
4 lb beef, chuck with bone	black pepper to taste
3 Tbsp red wine vinegar	4 Tbsp parsley, minced
1/2 lb smoked pork butt	1 cup potato, peeled, diced 1/2" cubes
2 Tbsp butter	1/2 cup sour cream

In a large stock pot bring the beef to a boil in 2 1/2 quart. Water with 1 tbs. of salt. After 10 minutes of boiling reduce heat and simmer for 30 minutes more, then remove meat, cool and remove meat from bone & cube 1/2". In a large skillet on heat the oil on medium heat. Saute the onion, beets, and carrot until they are soft. Add the potato and butter then cook for 2 minutes more. In the mean time bring the beef stock, water & beer to a boil in the stock pot. Add salt and pepper, vinegar, and meat. Drain the beet-carrot-onion and potato mixture and add to stock pot. Reduce heat and cook for 20 min. then add cabbage, tomato paste and pork butt. Cook another 30 to 45 minutes. Remove from heat and allow to cool to room temperature. Refrigerate overnight, reheat and serve. A large dollop or 2 of sour cream in the soup is mandatory when served.

Allow each person to stir it in themselves.

Note: You may add 1 1/2 cups of cooked white beans to this soup if you wish but if you do so soak them in vinegar then add them to the soup.

I like to believe that one day Borsch
will be as popular as Pizza!

Index

Printed in the United States
by Baker & Taylor Publisher Services